A WINTER'S TALE

BOOKS IN THE PUPPY PATROL™ SERIES

COMING SOON

A WINTER'S TALE

JENNY DALE

Illustrations by Mick Reid
Cover illustration by Michael Rowe

AN
APPLE
PAPERBACK

SCHOLASTIC INC.
New York Toronto London Auckland Sydney
Mexico City New Delhi Hong Kong Buenos Aires

ISBN 0-439-31908-0

21 20 19 18 17 16   16 17 18 19 20

Printed in the U.S.A.   40
First Scholastic printing, November 2001

SPECIAL THANKS TO CHERITH BALDRY

CHAPTER ONE

"Dick Whittington and His Dog?* What sort of play is that?" Neil Parker pointed to a brightly colored poster on the bulletin board and laughed. "What happened to the cat?"

"Who needs a cat?" his sister Emily said. "Denny's perfect. He's our star pooch."

Neil and his mother, Carole Parker, along with Neil's five-year-old sister, Sarah, had arrived at the church hall in Compton to pick up Emily from her rehearsal. Every year the Compton Amateur Dramatic Society put on a special Christmas show for the local children, and this time Emily had a small part.

Neil had first met Denny, the golden retriever in

the performance, when a truck had hit the dog on the road just outside King Street Kennels. Gina Ward, who was in the grade below Neil at Meadowbank School, had been walking Denny when the accident took place. Neil had helped her look after him while they waited for the vet. He didn't find out how clever Denny was until much later.

"Fudge is perfect, too," said Sarah. "Why can't he be in the play?"

"*Dick Whittington and His Hamster?*" said Neil. "In your dreams, Squirt."

"Hamsters are too small," added Carole as Sarah scrunched up her face and sulked. "No one in the audience would be able to see him."

Neil was fidgeting as he looked around. The weather was icy-cold outside, with snow expected, and the church hall felt distinctly chilly inside, even though Neil was wearing two sweaters, a padded jacket, *and* a cap with earflaps pulled down over his spiky, brown hair. He slapped his hands together in their woolen gloves.

Neil could hardly believe that the show would be ready in time for New Year's Eve — just ten days away, or that the cast had already been rehearsing for several weeks. The stage was empty except for a couple of chairs and a table. The people standing onstage were busy talking to one another, not even trying to rehearse.

At the other end of the room, C———— ———— two of Neil's friends from school, w—— ————— onto a big canvas. In fact, Meadowb—— ———— well represented; Neil's teacher, Paul ————, was there, too, perched dangerously at the t—— of a ladder, fixing one of the stage lights.

"Are you going to be long?" Neil asked Emily. "I want to get back home."

"I don't know."

Neil shifted again and looked at the hall clock impatiently. It was almost half-past five. "I've got to be home by six," he said. "Jane Hammond is bringing Jake over."

Before Emily could reply, somebody called her name, and she dashed off toward the stage. Neil turned back to where Carole was sitting on one of the chairs against the wall.

"Mom, I've got to be home by six," he repeated.

Carole was staring straight ahead, not noticing Neil at all. "I've mailed the last of the Christmas cards . . ." She ticked the item off on her fingers. "I've bought the turkey. I've bought the vegetables, the chocolates, and . . . gift wrap! I forgot the gift wrap!"

"Oh, Mom . . ."

Carole Parker picked up her handbag. "Neil, I'm just going to run down to Main Street before the shops close. Keep an eye on Sarah for me. I won't be long."

"Mom —" Neil protested, but Carole's tall figure was already disappearing out of the room.

Neil shrugged and looked around for his little sister. She was waving a brush around, trying to help with the painting but getting more blue paint on herself than on the scenery.

"Mom'll kill me!" Neil groaned as he looked at Sarah's paint-spattered jeans.

He walked down the hall to where the set painters were at work. Hasheem straightened up, making a face and rubbing his back vigorously.

"Here comes the Puppy Patrol!" he said. "Why aren't you in the show, Neil? There's a dog in it, you know. I didn't think *anything* could keep you away from dogs."

"You've got to be able to sing," Neil replied. Then he grinned. He was a little disappointed not to be in the performance, but he wasn't going to make a big deal about it.

"And your voice sounds like all the dogs in King Street Kennels howling at once." Hasheem chuckled. "That explains a lot."

Neil's parents, Carole and Bob, ran a boarding kennel with a small rescue center in the country town of Compton. The thought of the residents of King Street Kennels all howling at once was pretty scary.

Neil looked down. "So what's all this artsy stuff?"

"It's the road to London," Chris said, squatting

back and moving the hair out of his eyes, leaving a blue streak across his forehead. "You know, 'Turn again, Whittington,' and all that."

The canvas showed a road and some trees and blue sky, which Chris and Hasheem were filling in. There was a sign with LONDON 7 in big black letters.

"Dick makes friends with this stray dog," Chris explained. "In our case, with Denny back there." He pointed to a makeshift dressing room at the side of the stage. "Then the dog goes to London with him and makes his fortune."

Neil wasn't really listening; Emily had been talking about the show nonstop, and he knew the story backward and forward. He glanced up at the clock again. Twenty to six. "I'm going to be late," he muttered to himself.

Onstage, the actors and stagehands finished moving the furniture around. Gina's older sister, Beth, came out from behind a curtain and stood center stage. She played Dick Whittington, even though she didn't look much like it now, dressed in blue jeans and a sporty hooded sweatshirt. Her long fair hair was all over the place. Denny trotted onstage as well, and sat at Beth's feet. Everybody else walked off the stage. Neil suddenly became interested when he realized they were going to rehearse one of Denny's scenes.

Beth sat down at the table and pretended to be hold a pen. "Denny, we sold five shillings' worth of spices to Mistress Williams, and three shillings' worth to Master Snip, the tailor. Five and three, Denny — what does that come to?"

Denny, who had been listening alertly, barked eight times. Neil, who knew what to look for, saw the hand signal Beth gave him when he had to stop barking, but it was such a small movement the audience would never notice. They would see a dog that was bright enough to do math!

Everybody laughed and clapped when the short scene was finished. Beth stood up and took a bow, then patted Denny. The retriever looked pleased

with himself, his tongue hanging out in a wide doggy grin.

"I'm going to teach Fudge to count like that," Sarah announced.

Neil groaned again.

At last, the rehearsal was coming to an end. Mr. Hamley came down the ladder and Beth led Denny off the stage. Everyone else began collecting their belongings and putting on their coats. Gavin Thorpe, the minister, appeared at the door of the church carrying a heavy bunch of keys.

"At last!" said Neil. "Can we go now?"

"What's the rush?" Hasheem asked. "You've been squirming ever since you got here."

"I've got to get home. Jake's coming tonight."

Hasheem looked puzzled. "You never said you had a friend staying over for Christmas."

Chris laughed and took a swipe at Hasheem with his paintbrush. "Get real, Hasheem! Since when have you known Neil to be bothered about looking after his friends? Jake's a dog, you fool!"

Neil grinned at him. Chris Wilson was his best friend, and he'd heard a lot about Jake over the last few weeks. Jake was a Border collie puppy — the son of Neil's beloved dog, Sam, and another Border collie named Delilah, who lived at the neighboring Old Mill Farm. Delilah had a beautiful brood of five adorable pups — and now that Jake was finally old enough to leave his mother, he was coming to live with Neil.

Delilah's owner, Jane Hammond, had promised to bring ten-week-old Jake over at six o'clock that evening. It was one appointment Neil had no intention of missing.

He said good-bye to Chris and Hasheem, and with Sarah in tow, went to get Emily, who was giggling in a corner with her friends Gina Ward and Julie Baker. She grinned at Neil as he walked toward her.

"I told you Denny's perfect," she said.

"That's a great scene," Neil agreed, feeling a bit disappointed that he wouldn't be in the show. "You've trained him really well, Gina."

"It's Beth, really." Gina blushed. "He'll do anything for her."

"This will be the best show ever," Julie said. She laughed. "Do you think we should put Ben in it as well?"

Neil winced. Julie's Old English sheepdog, Ben, was the sloppiest and most loving dog you could hope to meet — and the clumsiest. Neil smiled as he pictured flying props, furniture tipping over, and scenery falling on top of a surprised but well-meaning Ben.

Then he stopped smiling. He had noticed the clock again. It said almost five to six — and where was his mother?

It was after six by the time the Parkers set off toward home in their green Range Rover with the King Street Kennels logo on the side. Neil was fidgeting with impatience in the front seat.

"Calm down," Carole told him. "Your dad's at home. Jane will wait for you."

"But I want to be there," Neil said. "Jake's mine. I want to welcome him."

The night was already pitch-black and cold, and snow had started to fall. Carole was driving carefully for fear of skidding. Snowflakes whirled in the beams of the headlights. In the backseat Sarah was bouncing up and down chanting, "I'm going to make a snowman! I'm going to make a snowman!"

"Shut up, Squirt," Neil muttered.

"When are we going to decorate the tree?" Emily asked. "Can we do it tonight? Sarah and I made some decorations."

"I made a big star," Sarah announced proudly.

"We'll see when we get home," Carole said. "We've got lots to do before Christmas, and this weather isn't helping."

Neil was very excited about the thought of his new puppy. Jake would be his to look after all the time now. It wasn't just fun, Neil knew. It was a big responsibility. Just as well that school had finished, and he would have the whole Christmas break to settle Jake into his new home.

As the Range Rover approached King Street Kennels, another car, coming from the opposite direction, turned in at the gate. Neil recognized the Hammonds' brown Volvo at once.

"There's Jane!" he exclaimed. "Great! We haven't missed her!"

As soon as their car stopped, Neil ran across the driveway and over to the Volvo where Jane Hammond was getting out. She was small and slim, with curly dark hair, and she wore a boxy jacket over a thick sweater and corduroys.

"Hi, Neil," she said, smiling. "All ready for the new arrival?"

"Sure!" Neil grinned back at her.

Jane opened the back door of the car and reached for a pet carrier on the seat. By this time the rest of the Parkers had joined Neil.

"Is it Jake?" Sarah asked, wriggling past Neil to peer into the back of the Volvo. "Can I see?"

"Let's get him inside," Carole said. "Then we can all see."

"Don't get in the way, Squirt," Neil said. "You're holding things up. Jake will get cold."

Jane gave the pet carrier to Neil to carry into the house. He could feel a small body shifting around inside it, and he heard a scrabbling sound. Against the mesh at the front of the carrier, he made out a black nose and two shining eyes.

Light flooded down the steps as the front door opened and the tall, broad-shouldered shape of Bob Parker appeared. "I thought I heard a commotion! Come inside, all of you — it's freezing out here."

Neil hurried inside with the pet carrier, squeezing past his father. Everyone crowded after him down the hallway to the kitchen.

Neil set the carrier down in the middle of the kitchen. His fingers were shaking as he undid the latch and let the door fall forward.

"Jake?" His voice was unsteady. "Come out, Jake. This is your new home."

A tiny black muzzle thrust itself out of the shelter of the carrier, followed by the rest of a black-and-white head with bright eyes and silky ears. Black paws propelled the rest of the puppy a pace or two into the kitchen were he stood watching Neil, who had squatted down in front of him.

"Jake?" Neil repeated. "Hi there, Jake."

The tiny puppy looked alertly at the others who stood around him, and then back at Neil. He advanced another step and nosed Neil's outstretched

hand. His little tail suddenly began wagging frantically.

"He remembers me!" Neil said delightedly. "He knows who I am." He looked up at Jane, who stood smiling down at him. "Thanks, Jane. This is really going to be the best Christmas ever!"

CHAPTER TWO

Sarah reached out to pet the puppy, but Carole quickly caught her hand.

"Not just yet," she said. "Give him time to settle in first."

Jake started to move away from the pet carrier, nose down on the kitchen floor and tail in the air as he tried to make sense of this exciting new place. Neil watched. He knew he had a silly grin on his face and he didn't care.

"Coffee, Jane?" said Carole, above his head.

"Please. It's arctic out there, isn't it? The snow's already sticking on the road down to the farm. That's why I was a little late." She took out an envelope and handed it to Carole. "Before I forget, there's Jake's vaccination certificate. He'll need a second shot in about a month, but you know all about those things."

"I've been reading about it," Neil piped up. "If he's not vaccinated, he could get distemper and hepatitis and . . . oh, I've forgotten the others."

"Poor Jake!" said Sarah. "All those needles stuck in him!"

Bob laughed. "No, dear. It's all in one injection. Though there is another vaccine against kennel cough. He'd better have that, too, because he's bound to come into contact with the boarding dogs when he's a little older."

Neil nodded, not taking his eyes off the puppy. Whatever Jake needed to grow into a happy, healthy dog, Neil would see to it that he had it.

As Jake was exploring the kitchen, he came close to the basket where Sam would usually be napping. Jake sniffed the blankets inside.

As if on cue, Sam padded into the room, disturbed from his cozy spot in front of the living room fire by the noise everybody was making.

"It's Jake's dad!" Sarah clapped her hands vigorously.

Sam sat beside his basket and watched the young puppy exploring his new surroundings.

"Do you think Sam knows that he's Jake's father?" Emily asked.

Neil held out his hand to scratch Sam's ears. "I've

been reading about that, too," he explained. "Dogs don't really know about families like we do. Wild dogs live in packs, so that's how they think. Sam was here first, so he's the pack leader. That means we have to show Jake that Sam's the boss."

"How do we do that?" Emily asked.

"Oh, it's easy. Feed Sam first, pat him and praise him first if they both come to you." He scratched Sam's ears again, smiling affectionately. "Jake's terrific, but Sam can't feel left out."

Sam had been Neil's dog for years, ever since he had been found as a puppy, abandoned and wandering by the old Compton railway line. Until recently, he had been a champion in local Agility competitions. But just a few weeks ago, at the same time that Jake was born, they had discovered that Sam had a heart murmur. Even though he was still a happy, healthy dog, there would be no more Agility contests for Sam. He had to take it easy from now on.

Neil laughed as Jake put his paws up on the edge of the basket and sniffed curiously at Sam. Sam bent his head. Father and son touched noses.

"Aren't they sweet!" said Emily.

"Hey!" Neil said as Jake's hind feet scrabbled against the basket. The pup was trying to climb in, and Neil wasn't sure how Sam would take the invading of his territory.

Neil gently pushed Jake away. Carefully he picked

him up with one hand under his chest and the other supporting his hindquarters, and carried him across the kitchen.

"This is *your* basket, Jake," he said.

For now, Neil had brought in one of the plastic beds that they used in the rescue center, and padded it with warm bedding. Puppies always chew their beds, and letting Jake chew a regular basket might hurt him since he was still so tiny.

Next to the bed were two big bowls. Neil put Jake down in front of them and filled one of them with water. Jake stuck his tongue in for a big drink.

"Isn't he small?" Sarah said.

"He'll grow!" Neil protested.

"He's very young," Carole explained to Sarah. "But he'll grow. You just wait!"

Sarah gazed at Jake as if she expected him to grow right in front of her eyes. "Aren't you going to feed him?" she asked.

"Give him a small meal later on," Jane suggested. "He's on four meals a day: two of puppy food with milk, and two of minced meat mixed with brown bread — cornflakes now and then for variety. I've been putting a teaspoonful of bonemeal and one cod-liver oil in one of the meat meals."

Neil nodded, taking it all in.

"I've brought some of the puppy food we've been using," Jane went on. "You can change to your own once he's settled in."

Sarah was still watching Jake as he drank. "I want a puppy for Christmas," she said.

"You always want a puppy!" Neil laughed.

"You're too young to look after a puppy on your own," Carole explained. "but I'm sure Neil would like some help with Jake once he's settled in."

"You're just a pup yourself, Squirt!" said Emily.

Neil didn't say anything.

"Besides," said Bob, "remember that a puppy's for life, not just for Christmas." Every year the Parkers had to find new homes for puppies that had been given as Christmas presents and then abandoned by owners who couldn't care for them. People just didn't realize what a responsibility a puppy could be.

As Jake finished his drink, Carole said to Neil, "You should really take him outside after that. But it's so cold I've put some newspaper down by the door. Use that for now. Just bring him over there and see if he gets the idea."

Neil did as his mother suggested, but Jake immediately bounced off the newspaper again. Neil put him back. Jake gave him a look as if he wanted to say, "What's all this about?" but after a minute he squatted down and produced the expected puddle.

"Well done, boy! Good dog!" Neil praised him, while Sarah jumped up and down and clapped as if the pup had done something really clever. Maybe he had; it was better than in the middle of the floor. All the same, Neil thought as he picked up the soggy newspaper, he'd be *much* happier when it was warm enough for Jake to go outside.

When Neil went downstairs for breakfast the next morning, Jake was romping around the kitchen.

After feeding Sam and then the puppy, Neil sat down for his own breakfast. Just then, Bob Parker came in through the back door in a swirl of fluffy snow.

"Shut the door, Dad!" cried Emily, already seated at the table. "You're letting the warm air out."

"Yeah, and think of Jake! He'll catch a cold!" Neil warned, fixing himself a bowl of cereal.

The puppy danced around Bob's boots, sniffing the sludgy snow as it fell to the floor, seemingly oblivious to the icy blast.

Bob unzipped his thick winter jacket and stomped his feet on a mat. He nudged Jake back toward his basket. "Sorry, but it's absolutely freezing out there — I had to come inside again for a minute to warm up. I've been chipping the ice off the barn doors. They're almost impossible to open."

Neil looked up. "Is it that bad?"

"Worst I've seen for a long time. Make sure you've got decent boots on if you go out. The snow is already fairly deep between here and the kennel blocks. I hope it doesn't go on too much longer or we'll have trouble keeping things running."

Emily laughed and pointed toward a pile of mail

on the table. "Anyway, if the mail's still being delivered it can't be that bad!"

Neil flipped through the pile. Most of the letters were for Bob and Carole, but there was a copy of the animal magazine that Emily subscribed to, and one large white envelope for him. Neil ripped it open.

"Hey, great," he said. "Look, it's a card from Max and Prince." Quickly he read the few lines scribbled inside the card. "Max says they're filming up here again in the new year. He might be able to drop in and see us."

Max Hooper, with his dog, Prince, was the star of the Parkers' favorite TV show, *Time Travelers*. Not long ago, Neil and Emily had been extras in an episode taped at nearby Padsham Castle. Neil and Max had kept in touch ever since, and Neil was delighted at the thought of seeing his friend again. He was sure Max and Prince would love to meet Jake.

Carole had served up eggs and bacon, and was now looking through her own holiday cards.

"One from Mr. Bradshaw and Marjorie," she said, passing it over to Bob. "And one from Eddie and Maureen Thomas, and Blackie — look at the pawprint! And a calendar from Preston's — Bob, that reminds me. Did you find out when they'll deliver the dog food I ordered for the holidays? We'll be needing it before long."

Bob swallowed a mouthful of bacon. "I called them yesterday. They're having trouble fitting in all the deliveries before Christmas, but they promised me it would be here by tomorrow at the latest."

"I'll believe it when I see it," Carole said.

After breakfast, Neil got ready to help with the kennel work.

"Don't forget to bundle up warm," said Carole. "The snow didn't let up overnight."

When Neil opened the back door, he saw the courtyard covered with a layer of white, already crisscrossed by lines of footprints from the kennel blocks to the house, the barn, and the separate block that housed the rescue center. Thin, wispy flakes of snow fluttered down and swirled all around.

Neil pulled his hat down over his ears and launched himself into the snow.

In the storeroom he found Kate McGuire, the kennel assistant, measuring out the food for the boarding dogs. Her fair hair was tied back, and she was wearing some thin thermal gloves.

"Hi!" Neil said. "Jane brought Jake over last night. Are you coming to see him?"

"You bet," Kate said. "Just as soon as I've finished here. This is the last batch." She dug the scoop deep into the sack of dog food. "We're running low. I hope we get that delivery before Christmas."

"Tomorrow, Dad said," Neil told her. "Do you want me to take these in?" He nodded toward the bowls.

King Street Kennels had two kennel blocks, with

the storeroom between them. Each of the blocks had
two rows of ten pens, with an aisle down the middle,
and each pen had its own separate exercise run. Today, though, the doors to the runs were closed, to
keep out the cold.

As Neil opened the door of Kennel Block Two, a
blast of warm air greeted him. The blocks were
heated during the colder weather by pipes running
through the concrete floor; his dad must have turned
the heating up.

The frantic barking of the last few hungry dogs
sank to a contented snuffling as they pushed their
noses into their bowls. With the job done, Neil took a
few minutes to talk to the dogs. Some of them had
been regular visitors to King Street for years.

"Hello, there, Bundle," he said, stopping in front of
a hairy mongrel that had spent some time in the rescue center. The last time Bundle was at King Street,
he was bright pink — the result of a cruel practical
joke. "You're looking good."

He slipped Bundle a dog treat from the supply he
always carried in his pocket. Next to Bundle was
Flora, a Jack Russell that was a regular visitor, and
next to her a Welsh corgi named Taffy.

The pen at the far end of the block had been empty
when Neil went out the day before. Now it was occu-
pied. Neil peered in to see one of the biggest dogs
he'd ever seen, sitting and looking back at him with
a sorrowful expression in his liquid brown eyes. The

dog had a shaggy brown-and-white coat, with a white muzzle and chest, and black shading on his face and ears.

"A Saint Bernard!" Neil exclaimed. "Wow, you're massive, aren't you?" He held out a treat through the mesh, half afraid that the enormous dog would swallow his fingers as well.

Neil heard Kate's footsteps approaching him down the aisle.

"What's his name, Kate?" asked Neil.

"Bernie. His owner left him here yesterday, while he goes off to Spain for some winter sun." She flicked some snowflakes off her shoulders. "Can't say I blame him."

"But it's warm in here. Anyway, if one of us gets lost in the snow, Bernie can come and find us."

Kate laughed. "Don't bet on it. His owner, John Cartwright, used to train dogs for the mountain rescue service before he retired. He told me that Bernie was the only dog he'd never been able to train at all."

Neil stared at the Saint Bernard again. "He's never saved anybody?"

"Not one."

Huh, Neil thought, I bet I could train him! Then he stopped himself. He better not get too big-headed. John Cartwright was a professional, after all, and if he couldn't train Bernie . . . Neil gave the big dog a last glance as he followed the others out of the kennel block. All the same, he thought, I'd like to try.

As Neil crossed the courtyard again, blowing warm air into his gloved hands, he looked through the side gate and saw a blue minivan turn into the driveway. The car glided silently to a halt on the deepening snow and Gina Ward scrambled out almost before it had stopped. Neil walked over to meet her.

"Hi," he said. "Have you come to —"

He broke off, noticing her tears. "Neil, it's awful!" she said. "We've lost Denny!"

CHAPTER THREE

"Lost Denny?" Neil echoed. "What do you mean? How?"

"I don't know." Gina twisted the ends of her scarf worriedly. She looked very upset. "He went out in the yard this morning, and when I went to call him in, he was gone!"

"Are you sure he isn't hiding?"

While they were talking, Gina's sister, Beth, got out of the driver's seat and came over to join them.

"Have you seen our yard, Neil?" she asked. "A mouse couldn't hide in there, never mind a dog the size of Denny. I found a loose plank in the fence. I think he must have squeezed out that way."

"Have you tried following his paw prints in the snow?" Neil suggested.

Gina shook her head. "It was no use. We could see his prints in the yard, but too many people had been up and down the street outside." Gina looked up at the white snowflakes drifting down all around them. "Maybe the snow confused him. It's the first time he's seen it piled up so high. Everything looks so different — even our yard."

"I called the police," Beth said, "but they haven't heard anything yet. They suggested that we get in touch with your dad."

That didn't surprise Neil. Stray dogs in and around Compton often ended up at the King Street rescue center. Neil had lost count of how many frantic owners the Parkers had reunited with their pets. He knew how Gina and Beth must be feeling, but there was nothing he could do to help them — Denny wasn't there.

"I'm sorry," he said, "but we haven't heard anything, either."

Beth shook her head. "I didn't expect you would have, really. I know you would have called us. But we had to give it a try. You will get in touch if he turns up?"

"Of course we will. You'd better give his information to Mom. And let's get inside — it's freezing out here."

Neil led Beth and Gina to the office. Emily had seen the car from the house and ran to meet them all at the door. She was shocked to hear that Denny was missing.

"What about the show?" she asked. "We can't do it without Denny. He's too important!"

"I know," said Beth. "And he's usually so good. I can't help thinking that something horrible has happened."

Carole looked up from her desk. "Don't say that. It's early yet. Let's not jump to conclusions, OK?" She sat Gina and Beth down in front of the desk and began to record Denny's information for the rescue center files. Neil and Emily crowded around to listen.

"He was definitely wearing his collar," Gina said. "It has a tag with his name and our phone number. So if someone *has* found him, why haven't they called? Only a thief wouldn't call."

"I know this is horrible for you, but you've got to stay calm," Carole said. "He's only been missing for two or three hours, and it doesn't do any good to think the worst."

Neil exchanged worried glances with Emily. Denny was such a clever dog, and so well trained, that if a thief knew about him he might think he could sell the dog for a good price.

"Have you seen anybody suspicious hanging around?" Neil asked.

Beth looked blank, and said that as far as she could recall there was nobody around when she let Denny into the yard that morning.

"Tell them about that phone call," said Gina, nudging her sister's arm.

Beth nodded. "Just two or three days ago I had an anonymous phone call. It was a man. He sounded very reasonable at first — asking me lots of questions about the show. Eventually he claimed we were being cruel to Denny by teaching him tricks and making him perform. He asked me not to use Denny in the show."

"What?" Emily snorted. "You don't have to *make* Denny perform. He loves it!"

"What did you say to him?" Neil asked.

"Nothing. I just hung up."

"And did you tell the police?" Carole made a note on the card where she had been writing.

"No." Beth shrugged. "I thought it was just some prank. But now I wonder whether he came and stole Denny to prevent him from being in the show."

Everybody was silent for a minute. Neil knew that some trainers were cruel to performing animals, and some kinds of animals were unhappy in captivity, but none of that applied to Denny. He was a happy, healthy dog, and Neil had seen at the rehearsal how he loved to show off. Even so, somebody who didn't know him might think he was rescuing him from abuse.

"I think you should report it to the police now," said Carole.

"Yes, I will." Beth glanced at her watch. "Come on, Gina. Emily, I'll see you later at the rehearsal."

"But will we be doing the show if Denny can't be found?" Emily protested.

"I don't know. But we can still rehearse. There are lots of scenes that Denny isn't in." She gave Emily a little shake and managed to smile. "Cheer up, Emily. The show must go on!"

"I've worked out a training program for Bernie," Neil announced at lunchtime. He sat at the kitchen table, carefully avoiding Jake, who was making little growly rushes at his feet.

"For Bernie?" Bob Parker gave his spaghetti sauce on the stove a last stir. "I thought you had enough to do, training Jake."

Neil felt himself going red. "Yes, well . . . I thought it would be a surprise for Mr. Cartwright."

"John Cartwright has been training dogs for years," Carole pointed out. "If he says Bernie is untrainable . . ."

"But there's no harm in trying," Neil said. "Em, you'll help me, won't you?"

Emily sat down and pushed her untidy dark hair out of her eyes.

"Not now. I've got a rehearsal. If I have time later, I might give you a hand."

"Sarah?" Asking for his little sister's help was a last resort for Neil — but probably better than nothing.

"I'm going to build a snowman!" Sarah said. "Fudge is going to help me."

"Thanks a bunch," Neil muttered. He was beginning to think that his attempt at training Bernie would have to wait.

"It's too cold for Fudge to be outside," Carole said as she began serving out the sauce. "But Neil's very good at building snowmen." She gave Neil a hard look. "Aren't you, Neil?"

Neil shrugged. "Oh, sure."

Bob chuckled. "And don't be too disappointed if Bernie doesn't cooperate when you *do* get a chance to take him out. I don't think snow and Bernie get along very well together!"

When Emily was at her rehearsal, Neil helped Sarah build a snowman in the courtyard during a break in the weather. He rolled a huge snowball for the body while Sarah made a smaller one for the head. She found an old hat and a scarf, while Neil raided the storeroom for dog biscuits to make eyes, a nose, and mouth.

Neil bent down and plunged his hand deep into a large, brown sack. Scrabbling around at the bottom, he pulled out a handful of dog biscuits and stuffed them into his jacket pocket. On his way out, he noticed that they really were getting low on dog food — there was probably only enough left to last a couple of days.

When he went back into the courtyard, he found Sarah rolling a third snowball.

"Not another snowman!" he protested. "I'm freezing. And it's getting harder to walk in this stuff!" Neil kicked a lump of snow on the ground.

"No, silly," Sarah said. "This is a snow-dog!"

They finished off the snow-dog with a curved twig for a tail and Sarah's scarf around its neck. She didn't want it getting cold. It didn't look like any breed of dog Neil had ever seen. Just as they had completed their sculpture, it started to snow again; big wet flakes that settled on the window ledge and the ground and the roofs of the kennel blocks. They had to leave the snowman and his dog, and take shelter. If the snow got much deeper, Neil thought, the Parkers might get cut off for Christmas.

As Neil went into the kitchen, something tiny collided with his foot. He looked down to see Jake trying to attack his shoe. Jake was really into feet. If you were that small, Neil thought, feet might be the most important thing you could see.

Grinning, he squatted down and tickled the little black-and-white pup on its tummy. "How about some training, Jake?"

Neil started by calling Sam over from his basket. The Border collie came promptly and looked at Neil with an alert expression.

"Now watch this," Neil said to Jake. He took out a dog treat, showed it to Sam, and said, "Sit!" Sam sat

at once, Neil gave him the treat and praised him.
"Now, Jake, do you think you can do that?"

Jake had watched with an interested look in his
bright eyes, but as soon as Neil took out another
treat, Jake started bouncing around, trying to reach
his hand.

"No!" said Neil.

He held out the dog treat to Jake, who sniffed it
while his little tail wagged excitedly. Neil lifted the
treat above his head, and Jake sat down to keep his

eyes on it more easily. He gave Jake the treat and played with his ears as the puppy wolfed it down.

Looking at Jake, Neil thought about Beth and Gina, who must have been missing Denny desperately. He wished he could do something to help. It would be a miserable Christmas for the Ward family without Denny.

CHAPTER FOUR

Neil knew how right he was when his dad brought Emily back from rehearsal. She was almost in tears.

"It was awful. Everybody was upset, trying to work without Denny. And Gina's really worried because Denny might freeze to death if he's out all night in this snow."

"It almost makes you hope he has been stolen," Bob said, taking his coat off. "At least a thief would keep him inside. It'll be bitterly cold outside tonight. If the snow keeps falling like it has been, I can see problems ahead."

He shook the melting remains of snow off his coat. Jake flinched and his paws skittered on the floor as one of the flying drops hit him.

"Hey, Dad!" Neil protested, scooping Jake up.

"Sorry, little fella." Bob grinned and rubbed Jake's muzzle with one finger. "Didn't see you down there."

"Maybe one of the dogs could track Denny," Emily suggested, cheering up a bit. "Maybe Bernie could do it."

"Not yet — I haven't worked my magic on him!"

"Modesty is not your strong point, is it?" Emily tried to hide a smile. "I think Jake could do a better job of tracking than Bernie."

Bob was still stroking the pup in Neil's arms. "Somehow I don't think so." He smiled sweetly at Jake. "He's got a lot of learning to do first."

Just then, Carole and Kate opened the back door and bustled into the warmth of the kitchen. Carole was holding holly covered in shiny scarlet berries. She laid it on the table carefully, then unwound her scarf and pulled off her wool hat.

"It's cold enough out there to freeze your feet off," she said. "Can you make me a hot drink, Bob?"

Bob rushed to the sink to fill the tea kettle. Kate took off her gloves and blew on fingers that were pink from the cold.

"It's at times like this," she said, "that I dream of a job in a nice, warm office."

"No!" Emily protested. "You can't!"

Kate laughed. "I was only joking. I don't really. But the snow's getting worse. We'll need skis to get across the courtyard tomorrow."

Neil looked out of the window again. A white veil of snowflakes whirled against the darkening sky.

"Maybe we'll be snowed in," he suggested. "That would be so cool!"

His mother gave him one of her looks. "If we are, you'll soon be wishing I'd shopped for more food. Feeding you all is like feeding an army on the march. Not to mention the dogs!"

Bob poured tea into mugs and handed one to Kate. "You're never going to be able to ride your bike home in this."

Kate wrapped her hands gratefully around the steaming mug. "No need to worry. Glen said he would pick me up."

"Good," said Bob. "And I really don't think you should try to come in tomorrow."

"But the dogs still have to be looked after," Kate objected. "It's harder work when the weather's like this."

Bob shrugged. "We'll cope. But if it keeps on snowing, you might not be able to get here. And if you do, you might not be able to get home again. That would really mess up your plans for Christmas."

"What are you doing for Christmas, Kate?" Emily asked.

"Spending it with Glen, of course," said Neil, grinning. "Look, she turned bright red!"

"Neil!" said his mother.

Just then the doorbell rang. Emily went to answer

it and came back with Kate's boyfriend, Glen Paget, his collar turned up and his long, fair hair plastered to his head with melting snow. He said hello to everyone and scratched Jake behind the ears. "Hi there, midget. I've heard a lot about you."

"Listen, Glen," Carole said, "tell Kate that she shouldn't try coming into work tomorrow. The snow's getting worse. It's not worth the risk."

"She's right, you know," Glen said to Kate. "It was hard enough getting here tonight."

Kate looked from Carole to Bob, and then back at Glen. Reluctantly, she nodded. "All right."

"And don't look so guilty," Bob told her. "Have an extra day's vacation, on the Puppy Patrol!"

"And have this," added Carole, taking a package wrapped in shiny paper out of a cupboard and presenting it to Kate.

Kate accepted it with a huge smile and thanked them. "I'm really sorry. I just hope you have a good Christmas."

"We will," Bob said. "And you enjoy yours, too."

"I'll make sure she does," Glen promised cheerfully.

As Kate and Glen were about to leave, Neil thought about Denny. Glen was involved with an animal rights group, and he might be able to shed some light on the phone call Beth had received.

"Glen," he asked, "do you know the Wards' dog, Denny?"

Glen shook his head. Quickly Neil explained about
Denny's talents, and how someone had called to tell
Beth she was cruel to make the dog perform. "And
now Denny's missing," he finished. "Do you know of
anyone who might have taken him?"

"To keep him out of the show?" Glen thought for a
minute. "That's a tough one, Neil. Some people don't
like to see performing animals, but a trained pet dog
is different from lions and tigers, which should really
be out in the wild. I can tell you this, nobody in my
group would steal a dog. I doubt that it's anything to
do with animal rights activists."

"It doesn't sound as if Denny was stolen," Neil said
when Glen and Kate had gone. He almost felt disappointed. At least an animal rights group would look
after Denny.

"So he might be wandering around in the snow,"
said Emily, gloomy again. "And they've canceled tomorrow's rehearsal. If someone doesn't find Denny
soon, there won't be any show."

In the excitement of Jake's arrival the night before,
they'd forgotten about the Christmas tree. Neil,
Emily, and Sarah decorated it in the living room after dinner. Sarah insisted on Bob lifting her up so
that she could put the glittery star she had made on
the highest branch. Carole kept the fragile orna-
ments out of Jake's reach, but the excitable little
puppy still managed to roll himself up in the tinsel.

"He's so sweet!" said Emily.

Carole was on her knees disguising the very ordinary bucket that held the tree with shiny Christmas paper. She stopped what she was doing to unwind Jake.

"You'll have to keep an eye on him, Neil," she said. "I hate to think what he would do if you left him in here by himself."

"Sure, Mom." Neil grinned and scooped Jake up to pick the last strand of tinsel out of his glossy coat. "Behave yourself, Jake, do you hear? And make sure you don't scare Santa Claus!"

"I think we should write to Santa and ask him to bring Denny back," Sarah announced.

"It's a little late," Emily said.

"Well, I'm going to!"

"You write if you want to, sweetheart," Carole said.

"The Wards couldn't hope for a better Christmas present, that's for sure."

On Christmas Eve morning, Neil woke up early. He looked out at the courtyard and the roofs of the kennel blocks covered with snow. There had been another heavy snowfall during the night, but now only a few flakes were drifting slowly down. His bedroom window was covered with frost patterns, and icicles hung from the gutter above.

The rest of the house was quiet. It would be a good time for a training session with Bernie. Neil would have to manage without any help, but at least there would be no one there to laugh at him.

He washed up quickly, and threw on jeans and a couple of thick sweaters, wondering what he could use to lay a trail of scent for Bernie. Then he had an idea.

He took the pillowcase from his pillow, fished some abandoned socks out from under his bed and put them in the case, then topped it off with a couple of shirts, a sweater, and some more socks from the laundry basket. That collection should have plenty of his scent on them. Satisfied, he tied a knot in the top of the pillowcase and tiptoed downstairs.

When he got to the kitchen, Jake was asleep, but Sam lifted his head alertly from his basket.

"No, Sam," Neil said. "Not now. It's way too cold for you outside."

When he had put on his boots and ski jacket, Neil took his bundle outside into the exercise field. On one side of the field the powdery snow had drifted so high that it came almost to the top of his boots, and his breath made clouds in the icy morning air. Starting near the gate, he dragged the bundle through the snow where it wasn't too deep, back and forth for a long stretch, and finally buried it.

"That'll do," he said to himself. "Let's see what he makes of that."

Neil opened the door of Kennel Block Two a crack and quietly walked inside. He didn't want to wake all the dogs — that racket would wake everyone else, and his mom and dad would be furious.

The air inside the block was warm, and the dogs were mostly still asleep. One or two raised their heads drowsily and watched Neil as he padded along the aisle between the pens.

When he reached Bernie's pen, Neil took the leash from the hook outside the door and went in. Bernie was snoring in a regular rumble that shook his whole body. Neil bent down and tugged gently at his collar.

"Come on, boy! Wake up!"

Bernie opened one drowsy eye and closed it again. His snores died away into a kind of hiccup, and then started up again. Neil gave him a gentle shove.

"Come *on!*"

This time Bernie woke up completely, thrust himself to his feet, and gave himself a shake. Neil grinned and slipped him a dog treat.

"That's better. Let's go, Bernie!"

As Neil led Bernie outside, he heard a high-pitched yapping from the Pomeranian in the nearest pen, and Bundle's deeper bark answering it from further down the row. *Go back to sleep*, he willed them silently, leading Bernie at a trot down the path and through the gate.

Once in the exercise field, Neil forgot about the other dogs. Neil pulled out one of his dirty socks that he'd stashed in his coat pocket and waved it under Bernie's nose. The dog's nostrils flared as he sniffed it. Then Neil unclipped Bernie's leash and let him poke around in the snow, trying to encourage him to find the end of the scent trail he had laid.

When Bernie reached it, he got very excited, snuffling around with his nose in Neil's footprints.

Neil crouched down beside him. "Seek, Bernie!"

Bernie nosed around again and finally came back to Neil and planted a huge, snow-covered paw on his chest. Neil staggered back, laughing.

"No, you silly dog! Other end . . . seek!"

Somehow, Bernie seemed to grasp the idea. He plodded back and forth along the scent trail, until he reached the pillowcase that Neil had buried, and scraped energetically at the snow to uncover it.

Neil stooped over him and gave him a big hug. "Awesome, Bernie! Well done!"

He fed Bernie a couple of dog treats and decided he would end the training session there. Next time, Bernie would remember he had done well. If I play with him for a bit, Neil thought, he'll want to try again.

They had ended up near the clump of bushes at the far end of the field. Neil found a stick and threw it for Bernie to fetch. The huge dog lolloped back and forth, scattering snow everywhere, enjoying the game just as if he were a puppy like Jake.

Neil checked his watch when snow started to fall again. It soon came down in multiple sheets of tingly,

wet drops and Neil quickly called Bernie back to him.

"Breakfast, Bernie?"

He was sure the Saint Bernard grinned at him. He clipped on the leash again and tried to lead him away but instead Bernie sat like a rock and yawned. Neil tugged the leash gently, and when Bernie still did not respond, he pulled on the Saint Bernard's collar. It was like trying to move a truck. "Up, Bernie! Come on! Just for me?" Neil beamed at the dog. "Please?"

At last Bernie heaved himself to his feet and tramped off up the field, with Neil striding alongside him, picking up the pillowcase as he went. As soon as Bernie reached the front gate, he flopped to the ground again.

Neil swung the gate open and motioned for Bernie to go through.

Bernie dropped his nose to his paws looking completely uninterested.

"I don't beg often, Bernie, but will you *please* come back to the kennel with me? The snow is going down my neck!"

The Saint Bernard's head swiveled to look at Neil, and then, with a ripple of muscles, he rose and plodded back toward the kennel. Already the snow was so heavy that Neil could hardly see the shape of the house and the kennel blocks, but as he drew closer, he could make out the figure of his father coming across the courtyard toward him. Neil broke into a run, with Bernie by his side.

"Dad!" He was panting as he reached him. "You'll never guess what Bernie . . ."

His voice died away as he saw his father's face. Bob Parker was hardly ever angry, but he looked angry now.

"Neil," he said, "what exactly have you been doing?"

CHAPTER FIVE

"Sorry?" Neil said, staring up into his father's eyes.

"I hope you are." Bob still sounded grim. He motioned for Neil to follow him across the courtyard. "Your mother and I were woken up at some ungodly hour by all the dogs barking their heads off —"

"Oops," said Neil.

"When we found out that Bernie was missing from his pen, the first thing we thought was that somebody must have broken into the kennel. Then your mother looked into your room and found you were missing as well."

"I'm sorry, Dad. I just thought it was a good chance to give Bernie a little training. And he —"

"You didn't think at all," Bob interrupted. He

stopped as they came to the door of Kennel Block One. When he spoke again he sounded less angry. "Neil, I know you meant well, but your mom and I have got enough to do today, especially when Kate isn't here, without having to look for a missing dog that isn't missing at all. I was minutes away from calling the police. Go and put Bernie back in his pen right now. And Neil . . . try to be more sensible in future."

After Neil had kenneled Bernie, he went back to the house and found the rest of the family having breakfast at the kitchen table. Sam and Jake were both looking on optimistically. Neil stamped snow off his boots.

"That smells good," he said, sniffing appreciatively as Carole dished up sausages and bacon.

"Consider yourself lucky that I didn't give yours to Jake," Carole said. "Sit down and . . . Neil — what in the world is *that*?"

Neil was still carrying the pillowcase full of clothes that he had used to lay the scent trail for Bernie.

"It's just clothes and stuff," he explained. "I used it to —"

"I bet you've been playing soccer with it!" Carole said. "Neil, just look at it! That was a good pillowcase."

Neil looked closely at his bundle for the first time since Bernie had dug it up. He had to admit it was filthy, and it had gotten torn. Still, in Neil's opinion, it was worth it if it had helped to train Bernie.

"You see, Mom —"

"I don't want to know." Carole sounded exasperated. "I really don't. Just take it upstairs to the laundry basket, and then come and have your breakfast."

The snow kept on falling. By the time breakfast was over, the footprints Neil and his dad had made in the courtyard were filled in again.

"I'm glad I finished the Christmas shopping," Carole said as she cleared the table. "I wouldn't want to drive in this."

Bob got up, nodding at Neil and Emily. "Come on, you two. Feeding time."

Without Kate, it took longer than usual to make up the food for the boarding dogs. Bob measured out the different diets, while Neil and Emily transported the bowls of food and water to the two kennel blocks and the rescue center. Carole stayed indoors to work on the Christmas preparations.

"To think I ever wanted snow!" Neil groaned, slipping and narrowly saving the food bowl he was carrying. Even in gloves his fingers felt like icicles. The falling snow was so intense he could hardly see across the courtyard. He couldn't help wondering what would happen to Denny if he was out in this weather. There had been no word from Beth or Gina since the day before, and Neil could imagine how they must be feeling.

When the feeding was done, Neil and Emily went back into the kitchen where Carole had hot drinks ready. A tray of muffins had appeared on the kitchen table. Neil reached for one.

"Hands off!" Carole swatted him. "They're for tomorrow."

"Quality control, Mom," Neil protested.

To avoid any more arguments, Carole put a box of chocolate cookies on the table. "Is there any sign of the dog food?" she asked Bob.

"No, I'm starting to wonder if the delivery van will be able to get through. I'm going to give Preston's a call." Bob drained his mug and went out into the hall.

Emily said, "Is there any news about Denny?"

Carole shook her head. "I would have told you if there was. Try not to worry, love. He might have found shelter somewhere."

She meant to be comforting, but she still sounded anxious. Everybody knew the danger Denny was in. Even watching Jake's antics as he tried to chase his own tail couldn't cheer Neil up. And he couldn't think of anything more that they could do.

When Bob came back, he was looking worried as well, but for a different reason.

"I got through to the delivery manager and he told me the snow had messed up all their schedules. It's only to be expected, I suppose. He said he'd try to get a van through to us, but he couldn't promise."

"Well," Carole said, "we've got food for a couple of days. Let's see . . ." She started counting on her fingers. "Today's Thursday. Christmas Day and then . . . Bob, if they don't deliver today, there won't be another delivery until next Monday."

"What are we going to do? asked Neil.

"There's the Cash-and-Carry on the other side of Compton," Carole said. "It'll be expensive, but we could buy a few cases of canned dog food there, and biscuits."

"Getting there's the problem," said Bob. He straightened up. "Let's wait until lunchtime. Then we'll decide. Neil, come and help me clear the driveway so we can get the car out, and if the Preston's van arrives, it can get through."

By the end of the morning, Neil's back was aching from shoveling snow, and he was sweating inside his padded jacket. More snow was falling all the time, so he couldn't help feeling that all his efforts would be wasted. But he and his father had cleared a path from the road to the house, and Bob had put down some of the straw that was used for the dogs' bedding, to help wheels get some traction.

"If the snow stops," Bob said, "we'll clear some of the exercise runs. That way the dogs can get out for a bit."

"Fantastic." Neil grunted. He never wanted to see

another shovel for the rest of his life. "Can we go in now? I've still got to wrap presents."

"Better do it later," Bob suggested. "When Sarah's in bed. She won't give you a minute's peace, otherwise."

Neil grinned.

Neil and Bob took the shovels back to the storeroom. On the way, they met Emily and Sarah plodding back through the snow from the rescue center.

"We've been checking up on the dogs," Emily explained. "They're really restless because they haven't been outside. We played with them for a bit, but Sarah wanted to play with Jake."

"Look for her Christmas presents, is more like it." Neil smirked.

"We'll try to get them out this afternoon," Bob promised. "Otherwise there'll be a lot of very messy pens to clean out."

Emily made a face. "There already are!"

Carole was in the storeroom when Neil and Bob put away the shovels.

"I've made a list," she explained, waving it, "of what we really can't do without. If Preston's doesn't turn up, I'll go to the Cash-and-Carry after lunch."

Hearing the word *lunch* reminded Neil that he was starving. He led the way across the courtyard to the house. Halfway there, he was met by Sam, padding through the snow and waving his tail cheerfully.

"Oh, Sam!" Neil exclaimed. "Don't tell me you've learned how to open the back door!"

He was leading Sam back indoors when a dreadful thought struck him: Where was Jake? He hurried into the kitchen. It was empty. Though Neil looked under the table and in the spaces behind the fridge and the oven, there was no sign of the vulnerable little puppy.

Neil ran out in the foyer.

"Jake! Jake!" he called anxiously into the emptiness.

No little puppy scurried up to answer him. Everything was quiet. Neil quickly checked the living room, the dining room they hardly ever used, the closet, and the bin under the stairs. Nothing. Emily tried to ask him what he was up to but he rushed past her into the kitchen without answering.

"Jake! Jake, where are you?"

Carole caught up with Neil first. She took one look at his panic-stricken face and asked, "Neil! What on earth is wrong?"

"Mom! Dad!" Neil gasped out frantically, resisting their efforts to calm him. "Jake's missing. I can't find him anywhere!"

CHAPTER SIX

"**C**ome on now," Bob said. "He must be around here somewhere."

"I've looked everywhere," Neil said. "He must have gotten out. I think Sam opened the back door."

"I doubt even Sam's clever enough to do that," said Carole. "But one of us might not have shut it completely."

"Jake loves exploring," Emily said, worried.

Neil headed for the door. "He'll freeze out there!"

"Hang on," said Bob. "Let's make sure he isn't here, first."

"I said I've looked."

"So let's look again."

Neil felt frustrated at the methodical way his father started checking the downstairs rooms again, and then upstairs, even though Jake hadn't learned to climb stairs yet.

Neil ran outside into the courtyard with Emily. He looked at the ground to see if he could find paw-prints leading away from the back door — but a busy morning of people tramping back and forth through the snow made it difficult to see anything clearly. Any marks that might have been tiny paw-prints were rapidly filling up with snow. It was useless.

"Where do you think he'd go?" Emily asked.

"I don't know. He really hasn't been out yet. He doesn't have any favorite places."

Neil and Emily began to search the courtyard, calling for Jake. Neil was frightened that the puppy might have gone out onto the road, but he realized that that was unlikely. He would have seen Jake if the pup had come out while he and his father were shoveling snow in the driveway, and they had closed the side gate carefully when they had finished.

The doors of the kennel blocks and the rescue center were all firmly closed to keep the heat in. Red's Barn was closed as well, but Bob had been in and out getting straw, and Jake could have slipped in then. Neil and Emily continued to search.

The barn was a wonderful place for a little dog to play and hide, but after a few minutes they were sure Jake was not there, either.

When they left the barn, they saw Bob coming out

into the courtyard. "Any luck?" he called over to them.

"No," said Neil. "Let's try the yard."

The whole time Neil was trying to push down the sick feeling in his stomach, desperately hoping that he would see the little black-and-white Border collie come bounding toward him through the snow. He wondered how long Jake had been outside. He knew Jake would freeze to death if they didn't find him soon.

There was still no sign of the puppy when they came to the field gate. Through the swirling snow Neil could just make out the hedge that separated their land from the Hammonds'.

"Do you think Jake tried to go home?" he asked Bob.

"To Old Mill Farm? I doubt it. Jane brought him here by car. He wouldn't know the way across the fields."

"We could call Jane, though," Neil suggested.

"She'll call us if Jake turns up. I don't want to worry her. Not yet, anyway."

Emily pushed open the gate into the field. "He could have come through here. Sam used to get through the hedge when he went to visit Delilah. Let's start looking."

Neil bit back a groan. The field was huge! If Jake was wandering around, they could easily miss him in the snow. The idea crossed his mind that he might get Bernie to track Jake, but he had to face up to the fact that he hadn't made any real progress with the dopey Saint Bernard. Not enough to risk Jake's life to his tracking skills.

Neil started calling again, working his way along the hedge, poking into the bushes with a stick to see if Jake was hiding. Snow spattered from the branches to the ground as he disturbed them, but there was no Jake.

Eventually he reached the clump of trees and bushes at the far end of the field.

"Jake! Jake!"

For a few seconds he heard nothing except his own panting breath. Then he thought that he could make out a faint whimpering. Emily came pounding up, skidded to a halt beside him, and grabbed his arm.

"Call again."

"Jake!"

This time Neil was certain. Jake had answered him. He plunged into the undergrowth, dislodging great masses of snow that slithered wetly onto his shoulders. Neil didn't notice. As he called Jake's name, the puppy's reply had become a feeble yapping.

Neil found him at last in front of a huge clump of brambles several feet from the fence. Trailing stems arched over, interlaced so they protected the ground underneath from some of the snow. He pushed back the curtain with one gloved hand. Beneath it, Jake

was crouched on a carpet of snow and dead leaves. When Neil appeared, the puppy got up, staggered a couple of paces to sniff Neil's hand, and then collapsed again, shivering. Neil picked him up.

"Oh, Jake!" He was swallowing tears; he told himself that was stupid, now that Jake was found. "Jake, what have you been up to?"

Back in the kitchen, Neil wrapped Jake in a blanket and settled him in his basket in a warm spot by the stove. He was still limp and shivering. Carole quickly heated some milk for him.

Moments later, Neil was crouching down beside

Jake and offering him the bowl of warm milk. The puppy lapped at it feebly and then closed his eyes.

"He's sick," Neil said anxiously.

"He just needs to warm up," Carole said. "Let him rest for a while."

Neil tried to help his parents with the kennel work, but he was distracted.

Looking in on him for the umpteenth time, Neil was still worried. Jake wasn't quite asleep. He kept twitching and whimpering, and he didn't want his milk.

Neil dragged his father back into the kitchen for a second opinion. "I think we should take him to see Mike," Neil said.

Mike Turner took care of all the dogs from King Street Kennels. Neil knew that if there was anything seriously wrong with Jake he couldn't be in better hands.

"Mike might not be at the clinic," Bob said. "It's Christmas Eve. And it'll be difficult to get there in this weather."

"It's stopped snowing," Carole said, overhearing their conversation as she stepped inside. "and the Preston's van hasn't turned up yet. If Mike is there, I could go to the Cash-and-Carry and take Jake over on the same trip."

Bob nodded. It was probably best to make sure the pup hadn't come down with anything serious.

Carole went out into the hall to call the vet.

Neil crouched anxiously over Jake, stroking his silky head. Sam came close and nosed his son, as if he was also worrying as well.

"Mike's there," Carole said as she came back into the room. "He'll see Jake if we go right away. He was just about to leave for the holidays — I just caught him. Emily, you'd better come with me and hold Jake on your lap."

Neil stood up. "Why can't I go? Jake's *my* dog."

"Because you'll be of more help here," Carole said.

"Your mother's right," Bob added, before Neil could protest again. "I need you here. If the Preston's van turns up, you'll have to help me carry boxes. There are still paths to clear, and the runs, and —"

"But I've shoveled snow all morning," Neil muttered rebelliously. "It's not fair."

"Neil," Bob said, "we had enough trouble from you first thing this morning. Don't be difficult now. Besides, which is more important, getting Jake to the vet quickly or standing here arguing?"

"I know . . ." It was hard for Neil to admit his dad was right. "You'd better look after him," he said to Emily as she slipped into her winter coat.

"Of course I will," she said sympathetically, swathing Jake in a blanket from his basket so that only his nose poked out of the folds. "I promise, Neil."

When Carole and Emily left, Bob let Neil take the dogs one or two at a time into the barn for some play and exercise, while he cleaned out the pens. It was just the sort of job Neil liked, and at any other time he would have enjoyed himself. Now he was just worried about Jake, and wished he could have gone with him instead of Emily. Sarah, however, was quite happy singing Christmas songs to the dogs.

"Time for a break," Bob said as he put back the last two dogs from Kennel Block One. "No sign of the Preston's van yet."

As Neil followed his father from the barn, the snow was falling again and refused to give up its relentless deluge of King Street Kennels and the Compton area. Huge feathery flakes were already piling up over the ground they had cleared that morning. The Range Rover's tracks from just a couple of hours before were already invisible. Sarah, clasping her dad's hand, was having trouble making her way through the deep blanket of snow.

"Mom's not back yet," Neil said.

Bob glanced at his watch. "She's been gone long enough." He frowned, and added thoughtfully, "Quite long enough to see Mike and then go on to the market. The snow must be holding her up."

"Or maybe there's something really wrong with Jake!" Neil said, panicking all over again.

"I doubt it," Bob said, reassuring him. He pushed open the kitchen door and Neil followed him inside, shaking snow off himself. "If you're really worried," his dad went on, "I'll try giving Mike a call."

With Neil at his heels, he went out to the telephone in the foyer and dialed the vet. Neil could just hear the faint ringing; it went on and on, until the answering machine cut in. Starting to feel desperate, Neil said, "Where is he?"

"The message says they're closed now until Monday," Bob said, starting to dial another number. "Which suggests that your mom made it to the clinic. Mike wouldn't have left when he knew she was coming. I'll try him on his cell phone."

He gave a nod to Neil when Mike Turner answered the call. "Hello . . . Mike?"

Neil could hear the speaker at the other end, but not the words he was saying. He shifted restlessly from one foot to the other and tried to make sense of his dad's end of the conversation.

"They did . . . great. And Jake? Yes . . . yes, I see. Fine." He stuck a thumb up and grinned at Neil who suddenly felt relieved. "And they left when? Oh . . . no, she was going to the Cash-and-Carry for dog food. Yes, I know . . . yes. It was?" Bob listened for a long time and then said, "OK, Mike, thanks. It's probably nothing to worry about. Bye . . . and Merry Christmas."

He put the phone down, frowning again.

"How's Jake?" Neil asked anxiously.

"Oh, Jake's fine. Mike says he was starting to perk up already by the time he got to the clinic. He was exhausted more than anything else. He just needs rest and warmth."

Neil felt a big grin spread over his face. "That's great!"

"Mike closed the animal hospital as soon as your mom left. He went home, and he tells me the snow-plows had been out on the main roads, so he didn't have much trouble getting there."

"Then where's Mom?" Neil asked. "Why hasn't she brought Jake home?"

"That's what I'd like to know," said Bob. "She's had plenty of time to get to the store. So where are they now?"

CHAPTER SEVEN

Neil and Bob stood in the foyer staring at each other. Then Bob shook his head.

"I'm losing my mind," he said, slapping his forehead. "Your mom took the cell phone with her. I'll call her on that."

He picked up the phone again and punched in her number.

Neil bit his lip.

Bob started to shake his head. "Nope. I'm getting a 'number unobtainable' message. The battery must have run out."

"So what do we do now?"

"Listen, Neil, I'm going to get back to work. There's nothing we *can* do stuck here. You stay near the phone, and give me a shout if your mom calls."

"And what if she doesn't?"

Bob frowned and tugged at his beard. "We'll worry abut that later. Come on, Sarah. Are you going to help me out again?"

When his father and Sarah had gone outside, Neil went back to the kitchen. After all the worry about Jake, he realized that he was starving again. He pulled off his jacket and boots, poured himself some milk and made a sandwich. Then he gave Sam a couple of dog biscuits. Sitting at the table, he ruffled the Border collie's fur.

"They'll be back soon, Sam," he said. "Everything'll be fine. You'll see."

Sam looked up at him, his eyes bright and trusting. Neil hoped that he was telling him the truth.

He hadn't been waiting in the kitchen long when Sarah skipped in, singing "Jingle Bells." The trouble was, she only knew the first line. You could have too much of anything.

"Do you have to keep singing?" Neil said in mock exasperation.

Sarah gave him a nasty look. "Don't be so rude. 'Jingle bells, jingle bells, jingle all —'" Her voice trailed off as if a thought had struck her. "Neil, will Santa be able to get here through all this snow?"

Neil sighed. "He drives a sleigh."

Sarah thought about this for a moment, and a beaming smile spread over her face. "That's all right,

then. I wrote to him and asked him to bring Denny
back for Beth and Gina."

"He might not be able —"

"Yes, he will! Santa is magical. He can do anything. 'Jingle bells, jingle bells . . .'"

To Neil's relief, his little sister skipped back outside to help Bob. Probably driving him crazy with
"Jingle Bells," Neil thought. All the same, he wished
she wasn't so confident. Her Christmas would be
spoiled if Denny wasn't found.

The sound of Sarah's footsteps had hardly died away when the phone rang. Neil ran out into the passage.

"King Street Kennels."

At first all he could hear was crackling. He raised his voice. "Hello . . . hello? I can't hear you."

Then words started to come through.

"Neil, it's Mom —"

Through the interference Neil could hardly recognize her voice.

"Listen, we're —"

"What?"

". . . battery's running out. We're —"

Neil gritted his teeth in frustration as the voice was drowned out in another wave of crackling. When it came back, his mom was saying, ". . . over the bridge and up the hill. Have you got that, Neil?"

"No!" Neil was starting to panic. "I didn't hear the first part. Where are you?"

Carole's voice came through again, obviously she was shouting, but hardly sounding any louder. "Can't get back . . . Emily's hurt, she —" More crackling. ". . . to help Jake."

"Jake?" Neil repeated, more alarmed than ever. "What about Jake? What's wrong?"

This time there was nothing but the crackling noise. The connection went dead.

He put down the phone and then tried calling his mother's cell phone number.

It was no use.

Giving up at last, he went outside to find his father.

Bob had no more success than Neil at getting through to the cell phone.

"She said Emily was hurt!" Neil kept repeating. "And something's the matter with Jake. She said something about helping Jake!"

He couldn't stop trying to make sense of the few scraps of news that had come through. "What are we going to do?"

Bob took a deep breath. "I'm going to call the police."

"But we don't even know where Mom is!"

"They can put out a call to all officers to look out for her. That's more than we can do, stuck here without any transportation." He started to call again. "Take it easy, Neil. Panicking won't help. In this sort of weather, a few cars are bound to get stuck here and there."

Neil couldn't bear to go on listening. He went back into the kitchen. The few words of his mom's phone call kept churning around in his mind. If only the battery hadn't failed! There was a spare in the office. She should have taken it with her.

Then Neil started to think. If his mom was stuck, if Emily was hurt and something had happened to Jake — Neil didn't let himself wonder what — she might not be able to leave them to get to a phone. What could he do to help her? If someone took them the spare battery, then Carole could call the police, or an ambulance, or a towing service for the car, or whatever she wanted. But there wasn't anyone to do it. Except me, Neil thought. And I don't know where she is.

He considered the garbled phone call again. His mom had said, ". . . over the bridge and up the hill."

The Cash-and-Carry was over on the other side of Compton, across the river and about as far as it could be from King Street Kennels. The route Carole would have taken was well used, and if she was stuck there she could easily have found someone to give them a lift or take a message. But she hadn't, so they were somewhere else. Carole must have had a reason to turn off the main road. Neil's mind was racing with possibilities.

On this side of the river was a whole maze of minor roads and lanes leading over the hills and dropping down again to rejoin the main road on the King Street side of town. What Neil's mom had said would make sense if she was up there somewhere. Neil swallowed and clenched his fists.

"I'm going to do it!" he said aloud.

Just then Bob came into the kitchen. Neil wondered if he'd heard, but all he said was, "Stay by the phone, Neil," and went outside.

Feeling like a thief, Neil crept down the hall to the

office and slid the spare phone battery into his pocket. As he was putting his jacket and boots on again, Sam came padding up to him. His head was cocked and his tail waved. Neil stooped down and patted him.

"Poor old boy, you've been stuck inside for ages. But you can't —"

He broke off and poked his head outside the back door. Since he had been indoors, the snow had stopped completely. A pale, watery sun had broken through the clouds, and the surface of the snow glittered faintly. Neil thought it wasn't as cold as it had been. He went back to Sam.

"OK, boy, why not?" he said. "It's not so bad out there now, and you could use a walk." Sam needed his exercise like all the other dogs, after all. "Let's go and find Jake, OK?"

Cautiously Neil emerged into the courtyard, with Sam following him on a leash. He couldn't see his dad, but he could hear barking from the rescue center, and he guessed Bob was in there. Swiftly he led the Border collie across the courtyard and out through the side gate. He didn't relax, or stop listening for his father's voice behind him, until he was down the driveway and out onto Compton Road.

Neil turned away from Compton, walked along the road for a little way, and then climbed over a fence leading to a path. That would take him in an almost direct line to the area he wanted to search. Sam hopped deftly over the fence reminding Neil of how good he had once been at Agility competitions. He stood next to Neil on the other side, tongue lolling, head up as if he was asking, "Which way now?"

The path itself was obscured by snow, but the outline of it, alongside a hedge, was easy to follow. From time to time there were small yellow markers intended for country hikers. Neil knew this terrain well, but it was almost unrecognizable under its thick coat of snow. He was thankful for the friendly dog trotting along beside him.

The smooth layer of fresh, pristine snow covered uneven places in the ground, so Neil kept stumbling into holes he could not see. Snow trickled down over the tops of his boots and slowly began to make his feet feel like lumps of ice. Once he slipped and fell. As he got up painfully, brushing snow off himself, he realized that he could get hurt. If he was stuck out here alone, probably no one would find him. He hadn't even left a note. For a few seconds he stood still, shivering and looking back. Had he done the right thing? Then, swallowing his fear, he went on.

His determination renewed, the going got easier as the path joined a farm road, where there were tire tracks for Neil and Sam to walk in. Before it reached the farm itself, another path led off to another fence and a lane. Its surface was unmarked; no cars had been along there recently, but at least it was more solid underfoot.

Neil felt a rising excitement. Now he was getting close to the area where he might expect to find his mom, Emily, and Jake. He led Sam uphill along the lane because they would need to cross the ridge of fields that surrounded Compton on this side.

They had not gone far when Neil realized that the sun was gone. Gray clouds were massing overhead again, and flakes of snow began to drift down, growing heavier with every step Neil took. He glanced down at Sam, padding undaunted alongside him.

"Thanks for sticking with me, boy. It won't be long now," he muttered.

As the bushes and trees on either side of the road thinned out, Neil became more conscious of the wind. It swirled snow in front of him. His eyes started to hurt as he tried to see his way. It drove snow into his face. His skin stung with it and his bare cheeks glowed bright red. He couldn't feel his feet any longer and his hands were starting to go numb. He wound Sam's leash around his wrist, in case he accidentally lost his grip.

After what seemed like hours — but was probably less than fifteen minutes — Neil realized that the upward slope was leveling out. They must be up on the ridge. He swallowed a gulp of snow-filled air and bent down to pat Sam.

Snow was matted in Sam's coat, but the Border collie didn't seem bothered at all. He gave Neil's hand a friendly lick and padded on into the wind. Neil began to wonder if he had been right to bring his dog.

Neil was finding it harder to see his way. The road stretched across the field, with nothing on each side but a ditch. A few steps later, he tripped over a cattle grid and barely saved himself from falling again. He kept veering from side to side, and only realized it when he saw the ditch open in front of him. Once he startled two or three sheep, huddling together in the shelter of rock. They ran off, bleating.

"Sorr-ee!" Neil cried after them.

Neil was so tired he could barely keep moving, but he knew it would be fatal to stop. People who were lost in the snow could lie down and go to sleep, and never get up again.

"We're not lost, are we, Sam?" he said, to comfort himself as much as the dog. "We know where we are."

He was beginning to feel really frightened, not for himself, but for Sam. How could he have been so stupid, to bring a sick dog out in weather like this? He should have known the snow would start up again. He peered around through the curtain of snow, but he could see nothing through the whirling whiteness. There was no shelter, and it was too late to go back.

As he kept going, Neil realized that instead of walking correctly at heel, Sam had taken the lead.

Instead of trying to guide them both through the snow, Neil started to follow. Right away, the going got easier. He just had to keep on putting one foot in front of the other, shield his eyes as best he could from driving snow, and let Sam find their way.

Soon they started to go downward again. They crossed another cattle grid, and gradually more bushes appeared by the road, sheltering Neil and Sam from the worst of the wind. It was easier for Neil to see, and he started to feel more hopeful — now he really might stand a chance of finding his family.

Not long after, they came to a crossroad. There was no sign to give Neil any idea of which direction to take. Sam seemed to want to go straight. Neil was too tired by now to do anything but let him have his way.

About a hundred yards down the road, Neil had to stop. In front of him was a tumbled wall of snow, reaching above his head. Neil wasn't sure where it came from — blown there by the wind, or abandoned by a snowplow, or deposited like an avalanche from the hillside above. He only knew that there was no obvious way around it.

"Bad idea, Sam," he said.

Together he and the dog slogged back up the hill. Going over ground they had already covered made Neil feel even more exhausted.

When he reached the crossroad again, he crouched beside Sam. The Border collie stood with his head down. His breath was coming fast, and Neil could feel a rapid heartbeat. It was vital to find a place for the dog to rest.

As he stood up, Neil realized something else. Although the snow was letting up, he could not see more than a few yards in any direction. Darkness was falling. The thought of how stupid he'd been hit Neil again. In the dark he wouldn't be able to find anything — not even his own way home.

"Left or right, Sam?" Neil asked. A lot depended on that decision. Sam just panted, obviously exhausted.

The left-hand road looked as if it led up to the field again. On the right, the road turned a sharp corner. Neil tugged on Sam's leash.

"OK, boy. Right it is."

This road twisted gradually downward. Finally Neil came to a place where it seemed to zigzag back on itself and start leading back up.

"Oh, no," Neil groaned. Was he ever going to get off the field?

He kept trudging on, Sam padding wearily at his heels. Then as he came to the next bend, he halted. After rising a little way, the road dipped again.

And below him, at the bottom of the dip, barely visible in the dying light, was the King Street Kennels Range Rover.

"Mom!" Neil yelled. "Emily!"

Energy flooded through him again. Slipping and sliding, he dashed down the road. Seeming just as excited, Sam bounded after him. The slope was so steep that Neil was only able to stop when he crashed into the side of the car sending a pile of snow sliding off the roof.

"Mom?" he said uncertainly.

The Range Rover was tipped forward, with its front wheels in a ditch at the side of the rod. The windows were frosty on the outside and misted up inside. Neil brushed snow off his face and scraped a circle of ice off one of the side windows. He tried to peer into the car, but he couldn't see anything.

"Mom!" he called, more loudly now.

He tried the driver's door, but it was locked. So was the rear door on the same side. Neil floundered through the snow around the back of the Range Rover. The ground gave way under him as he slid into a ditch. In his fall, he grabbed the handle of the rear door on the other side, and it swung open.

Apart from some crates of dog food, the Range Rover was completely empty. Carole and Emily and Jake were gone.

CHAPTER EIGHT

For a minute Neil stood and stared at the Range Rover. He couldn't think what to do. His plan didn't cover this.

He tried to figure out where his mom, Emily, and Jake might be. Maybe they'd left the car and tried to walk home, and that was how Emily had been hurt. But his mom surely had more sense than to try doing that in heavy snow, especially when they had a small puppy to carry.

More likely, Neil thought, they'd been picked up by the police or by a passing driver. Maybe they were safe at home now, while he was stuck out here. Neil groaned out loud. His mom and dad would be furious with him when he got back! But even that would be better than spending the night out here, and not getting home at all.

Neil used the car door to pull himself up out of the ditch. Looking around in the gathering darkness he saw a spot of something bright on the snow farther down the road. "Stay, Sam," he said.

Leaving the Border collie to rest by the car, Neil struggled down the road until he reached the bright object. When he picked it up, brushing snow off it, he saw it was Emily's red scarf. There were marks in the snow, too, though Neil could not make out what they were.

Just beside him was a gate; the snow was pushed away on the other side, as if someone had opened it recently. There were more marks on the hillside beyond, though the snow and the wind had partly erased them.

"Sam!" he called. "Sam!"

The Border collie came trotting toward him. Neil pointed up the hill. "Let's take a look, boy."

Sam squeezed through the space between the gate and the hedge, and scrambled away, scattering snow as he went. Neil climbed over the gate and struggled, floundering in deep, loose drifts.

"Sam, wait for me!" he shouted.

Suddenly Sam was there again, pawing eagerly at Neil's knees. Neil grabbed the leash. "You clever dog. What have you found?"

Sam let out a single bark, as if he was answering.

Looking up, Neil could make out the shape of a building, black against the darkening sky. Hope surged through him, and then died as he realized it wasn't a house, just a barn or a shed with blank walls.

"Sam, that's not —"

Neil's voice was cut off as Sam's bark sounded again, and as if in reply a light appeared ahead of them, by the dark building. Not light from a window; it looked more like a flashlight.

Neil took a few more steps, toiling up the hillside, feet slipping under him. Then he was flooded with relief as he started to make out the figure holding the light, and heard a voice calling, "Neil? Is that you?"

It was Neil's mom.

The barn was stacked with bales of hay. Carole had pulled some of them out to make a cozy nest where Emily sat with one leg stretched out in front of her. Jake was curled up asleep in a blanket on her lap. But what made Neil stand gaping, when Carole guided him into shelter, was the other dog, lying nose on forepaws, by Emily's side. It was Denny.

"You've found him!" he exclaimed. "Is he OK?"

"He's fine," said Emily. "He lost his collar somehow, but he's not hurt."

"But what happened? What are you doing here?"

"I could ask you the same question," Carole said. "Coming out in weather like this by yourself was

really dangerous. And bringing Sam — what if you'd gotten lost?"

Neil wasn't going to tell her how close he had come, up in the field. In fact, he felt so exhausted that he wasn't sure he could tell the story at all.

Carole must have seen how tired he was because she stopped asking questions, just nudged him further into the barn and closed the door tightly against the harsh weather outside.

"OK," she said. "Our story first. But you'd better have a really good explanation when it's your turn."

She switched off the flashlight to save the batteries and settled down in the hay next to Emily. Now the barn was dimly lit from windows high up under the roof. Neil collapsed on the floor on the other side of Denny. After so long out in the snow, the barn felt warm. Neil stripped off his gloves and pushed back the hood of his jacket.

To Neil's relief, Sam seemed none the worse for his struggle through the snow. He shook himself, scattering snow everywhere, and flopped down panting, his tongue hanging out in a satisfied grin. Neil grinned back, tired.

"Go on, Mom," he said. "What happened?"

Carole began by telling Neil about the visit to Mike Turner, and how Mike had reassured them that Jake would be fine.

"Then we went to the Cash-and-Carry. That was fine, too. We bought what we needed and set off toward home. And that's where our problems started.

"There must have been some sort of accident on the main road, because there was a line of cars stretching all the way back to the bridge. We spent about half an hour just inching along. So when we came to the turnoff onto the field, I decided to be clever and drive home by the back roads."

She swiped a hand across her forehead, pushing away straggling dark hair.

"It was fine at first. But the snow on the road was really thick, and even the Range Rover started to skid."

"And we ended up in the ditch," said Emily.

"So why didn't you stay with the car?" Neil asked.

"I was scared stiff when I found it and you weren't there."

"You can thank Jake for that," Carole went on. "Emily and I got out to see if we could push the car out of the ditch. Not a chance, of course. We left Jake in the back, and then before we knew what had happened, he'd taken off down the road."

"I ran after him," Emily explained. "And I fell and sprained my ankle." She tried to move the outstretched leg, and winced.

"We hope it's just a sprain," Carole said. "Anyway, I chased after Jake and I caught him just outside here. He was having a yapping fit. And just before I started to carry him back to the car, I heard another dog barking inside. I looked, and it was Denny!"

"Jake found him!" A beaming smile spread over Neil's face. "He's a real tracker dog!" He stared at the sleeping puppy. "I don't believe it!"

He guessed that Jake had just been feeling mischievous, but if his yapping had made Denny reply, that was good enough for Neil.

"So I helped Emily up here. I thought it would be warmer than the car," Carole went on. "That's when I tried to call, but the battery was too low. I could kick myself for not bringing the spare with me."

Neil felt a sudden warm flood of triumph. In all the confusion of the journey, he had almost forgotten about the cell phone battery, but now he pulled it out of the pocket of his jeans.

"You mean this?" he asked innocently.

Carole stared at it. "Neil . . . you didn't? That's un-believable! I thought we were stuck here all night, for sure."

She slid the cell phone out of the inside pocket of her jacket and replaced the dead battery. "Neil," she said as she punched in their home number, "I think you just got yourself out of trouble."

Neil grinned. A few seconds later he heard a voice at the other end as the phone was answered.

"Bob?" his mom said. "Yes, it's me. We're stuck in a barn somewhere. Neil found us and — oh." She flashed a look at Neil and handed him the phone.

"Neil, I've been frantic!" Bob's voice came through clearly. "You shouldn't have gone off like that without asking."

"But you wouldn't have let me go," Neil protested. "And Mom and Emily would —"

"I've got the police out looking for you, too!" his dad interrupted.

"Well . . ." Neil started to feel guilty. "I guess I could have left a note. But I'm fine, honestly, Dad. And you should have seen Sam! He —"

"Neil, put your mother on again. But don't think you've heard the last of this. We'll have a talk when you get home. A very serious one."

"OK, Dad. Bye."

Neil handed the phone back to his mom.

He was glad that he wasn't going home right away.

His dad probably needed some time to cool down —
but Neil wasn't too worried about getting a stern
talking-to. He was confident he had done the right
thing in setting out on his marathon journey with Sam.

Carole finished telling Bob what had happened,
and then called the police to ask for help. Not really
listening, Neil leaned over to stroke the sleeping Jake.

"Beth and Gina will be thrilled," he said to Emily.
"Do you think the show will go on now?"

"Yes, I guess so . . ." Emily's voice broke off, and
her eyes filled with tears. "but I'll be out of it now,
with this stupid ankle!"

"That's tough," said Neil. "I'm really sorry. Still,"
he added, "Denny's safe and that's the main thing."

Emily sniffed and nodded. "Yes, I know. But Neil,
there's something else —"

She was interrupted again as Carole put the phone
back into her pocket and said, "The police are on
their way. We'll be out of here before we know it."

"I hope so," Emily said. "That's what we haven't
told you, Neil. When Mom found Denny in here, the
door was shut. There was no way he could have gotten in by himself."

"You mean someone shut him in here?" Neil asked.

Carole nodded. "I don't know why, but it looks as if
somebody is keeping him here. And whoever it is, I
really hope the police arrive before they get back."

CHAPTER NINE

By now the barn was almost dark. Neil could barely make out the shapes of Emily and his mom or the dogs. Everything was quiet except for little scuttling noises in the hay, and an occasional snuffling from Jake in his sleep.

"Neil," Carole said, "do you think you could go down to the car and wait there for the police? They shouldn't be long, and I don't want to miss them."

"Um, sure," Neil said, groping to find the gloves he had taken off.

Before he could get up, they all heard footsteps scrunch in the snow outside the barn and someone whistling a tune. Then the footsteps and whistling stopped, and were followed by the sound of someone fumbling with the door lock. Emily audibly drew a breath. Neil felt his heart start to pound. He got to his feet, and his mom switched on the flashlight as the door swung open.

A man stood in the entrance, shielding his eyes from the light. He was tall, wearing a long ragged overcoat tied around his waist with tattered string. Even though there was snow on the ground, he wore scruffy sneakers, with holes in the toes. He carried a bulging plastic shopping bag.

Carole lowered the light slightly and the man took his hand away from his eyes to reveal sharp features pinched with cold, surrounded by a bush of straggly white hair and a beard. He was peering suspiciously at the Parkers.

"Who are you?" he asked. "What're you doing here?"

To Neil's surprise, it was Emily who replied. "Did you steal Denny?" she demanded fiercely. "The Wards aren't cruel to him. They're not!"

She tried to struggle upright and face him. Disturbed, Jake shot off her lap, yapping frantically, and hurled himself at the newcomer's shoes. Sam got to his feet, a low growling deep in his throat. Alarmed, the old man took a step back.

Only Denny stayed calm. He got up and trotted over to the man, who stooped and petted him, a smile spreading over his face.

"That's a good boy," he said. "Want to see what I've got for you?"

Neil started to realize that this wasn't an animal

rights protester, even one crazy enough to steal a dog to make his point. And anyone who was that fond of a dog couldn't be all bad. Neil told Sam to sit, and scooped up Jake before he could make any more holes in the man's sneakers.

"Emily, calm down." Carole had relaxed, as if she, too, realized that the newcomer was not a threat. "This dog belongs to some friends of ours," she told him. "They've been really worried."

"I didn't steal him, ma'am," the old man said. "I

found him wandering. He wasn't wearing a collar. I'd have taken him to his home if I'd known where he lived." He bent down again and scratched Denny's ears. "Denny's your name, eh? I called him Snowy," he explained, "'cause it was snowing when I found him."

"He had a collar when he got lost." Emily was still suspicious. "And you could have taken him to the police."

"There wasn't no hurry," the man said defensively. "Me and him, we found somewhere warm to stay, didn't we, boy? And then I went off to get us both something to eat."

He came farther into the barn and started to rummage around in his bag. From it he produced a soggy brown package and spread out the wrappings in front of Denny.

"There we are, boy. Nice bit of liver."

Denny started to eat hungrily. Sam showed no interest, but Jake wriggled in Neil's arms, yipping in a frenzy, and the old man, his wrinkled face creased into a smile, gave him a scrap of the liver in his fingers.

"He's a fine little puppy," he said. "Is he yours, son?"

"Yes, his name's Jake. I'm Neil Parker, and this is my mom, Carole, and my sister Emily."

The old man ducked his head.

"Pleased to meet you, ma'am. They just call me Nick. I didn't mean no harm, you know," he said to Emily.

Emily smiled, but Neil thought she still didn't look entirely sure that she wanted to trust Nick. Neil suspected that the old man was lonely, and might have been putting off the time when he would have to give Denny up. At least he'd kept him safe, when he might have died of cold.

"You can come with us when we take him home," he said. "The Wards will want to thank you, and —"

He was interrupted by the sound of a car engine laboring through the snow on the road at the foot of the hill. Blue light flashed on and off in the darkness outside the barn door.

"The police," said Carole.

Nick looked terrified.

"It's OK," Neil said. "We didn't call them because of Denny. Just to pull our car out of the ditch."

"I'll go down." Carole handed the flashlight to Neil. "You stay here where it's warm, and keep the dogs out of the way."

When she had gone, Nick started to unload more bits and pieces from his bag, as if he was going to settle in.

"You're not staying here, are you?" Neil asked. "don't you have anywhere to live?"

Nick shook his head. "I've been on the road for years. I wouldn't feel right no more with a roof over my head."

"But tomorrow's Christmas!" Emily protested.

Nick shrugged.

"You can't spend Christmas in a barn!"

Neil hid a quiet grin. The best way for Emily to stop being suspicious of Nick was for her to find out that he was in trouble. Emily couldn't resist helping — dogs, people, you name it.

"Why don't you come to stay with us for Christmas?" she continued. "Mom and Dad wouldn't mind, would they, Neil?"

Neil wasn't sure about that, but still . . . it *was* Christmas. "No, of course they wouldn't."

Nick frowned and shook his head. "Don't think I could do that. Wouldn't be right."

Another car engine roared in the distance. The Range Rover! Neil looked outside and saw the police van, its blue light whirling, and the Range Rover with its lights on. A policeman in a bright yellow jacket was walking between the two vehicles.

"They've set up a tow rope," Neil reported to Emily, who was trying to persuade Nick to change his mind. "The Range Rover's not moving, though. I wonder if —"

He cut himself off as the police van slowly moved backward, and the Range Rover lurched and almost leaped backward out of the ditch.

"Yes!" Neil said. "They've done it!"

He kept watching as his mom turned the Range Rover very slowly and carefully so that it faced the main road again. Then she got out and climbed the hill to the barn, closely followed by the policeman.

". . . so if you could help me get her into the car, I'll take her straight to our doctor," Neil heard her say as she came into earshot.

"No problem," the officer said, clapping his hands together. He was a huge young man with a friendly grin. "Good heavens, you've got a whole crowd here, haven't you?" the grin faded as his eyes fell on Nick. "Who's this? He's not with you, is he?"

"Yes, he is!" Emily said, flying to Nick's defense.

"I'm not doing any harm," Nick said. "Just sheltering from the snow."

"Well, you can't stay here, buddy," the policeman said. "This is private property. You'll have to move on."

"In this?" Carole said. "Oh, come on, officer. You're not going to throw somebody out into the snow on Christmas Eve?"

The young policeman looked uncomfortable. "I'm sorry, ma'am, but the law's the law. It's a fire hazard, for one thing, if he stays here. Come on. Let's go."

Muttering under his breath, Nick had already started to pick up his belongings into the plastic bag.

"Mom," Neil said, "this is horrible. Can't he come and stay with us for Christmas?"

"Please, Mom!" Emily added.

"Well . . ."

Carole was starting to smile, but the policeman interrupted her. "It's not a good idea, ma'am, if I may say so."

"No you may not," Carole said crisply. "Who I in-

vite into my house is my business. This gentleman
has already been very helpful in looking after our
friends' dog, and if he wants to come to stay with us
he's very welcome. Please come and spend Christmas with us, Nick."

Nick still looked doubtful, glancing from Carole to
the policeman and back again. Inspired, Neil said,
"We run King Street Kennels. We've got lots of dogs
for you to meet."

"You could give us a hand with them if you like,"
said Carole.

Nick's face lit up, and creased again into a pleased
smile. "Well, ma'am, if you're sure . . ."

"It's settled then," said Carole. "Now officer, if you
could just give Emily a hand, we can all get moving."

Everyone made their way down the hill slowly
toward the waiting cars. Carole went first, followed
by the policeman carrying Emily. Nick came next
with Sam and Denny padding after him. Last of all,
closing the barn door carefully behind him, came
Neil with Jake bundled inside his jacket. He wasn't
going to risk the little dog running off again.

The policeman helped Emily into the back of the
Range Rover, and went back to his own van where
another officer was waiting.

"I was going to take you to the emergency room,"
Carole explained to Emily. "But the policeman tells
me they've got a line a mile long. So I called Dr. Harvey, and he says that he'll see us at his home. He's

already closed for the holidays." Briskly she added, "Neil, can you get the dogs into the back? Nick, you can sit next to me."

When he was in the back of the car, surrounded by dogs, Neil leaned over and murmured into Emily's ear, "Don't you think there's something funny about this? Nick — Nicholas — bushy white beard . . . ?"

Emily started to giggle, but the engine starting up covered the sound.

"Better hope Squirt doesn't catch on," Neil added. "She always said Santa would bring Denny back!"

CHAPTER TEN

Dr. Harvey gently examined Emily's ankle.

"You've got a nasty sprain there," he said. "But that's all it is. I'm sure it's not broken. I'll put a bandage on it, and you've got to stay off the foot as much as you can for the next few days."

"Thank goodness it's nothing worse," said Carole.

The Parkers were huddled around the fireplace in Alex Harvey's sitting room. Finn and Sandy, the doctor's two dogs, lay on the hearthrug and watched his every move. Finn was a Kerry blue terrier, a real show dog, while Sandy was just an ordinary mutt. But now that the two of them had settled down together they were the best of friends, and Dr. Harvey loved them both.

Carole had left Sam and Denny in the car with Nick to look after them, but Neil had insisted on bringing Jake inside. The tiny Border collie scrambled around on his lap, eager to get down and make friends, but Neil kept him firmly out of the way. Finn could be a little temperamental at times. Besides, Neil didn't want to think about what Jake might do with a bandage!

"You've got a lively one there," Dr. Harvey said as he fastened Emily's bandage in place. He leaned over and tickled Jake. "Are we going to see him winning all the Agility prizes like his dad?"

"Maybe," Neil said.

"No, he's a tracker dog," Emily contradicted.

Dr. Harvey laughed. "Is he really? Isn't he a bit small for a bloodhound?"

"You could try training him for obedience *and* tracking events," Carole said. "But there's time enough to think about that when he's bigger. Let's get Christmas over first." She got up and started to put her coat back on. "Are you going away for Christmas, Alex?"

Dr. Harvey looked sad.

"I was going over to my sister and her family in York. But all the roads across the Pennine Chain are closed because of the snow. I'll never get there now."

"That's awful!" said Emily. She exchanged a look with her mother and Neil. "Mom, couldn't we . . ."

"Yes, of course we could. Alex, you're coming to have Christmas dinner with us. And Finn and Sandy, of course."

The doctor's face broke into a smile. "If you're sure . . ."

"No problem. Bob bought a turkey big enough to feed half of Compton. You're very welcome, Alex."

"Then in that case . . . ," Alex Harvey's grin widened, "we'd be delighted. All three of us."

"Great!" said Neil.

"Come about noon," Carole said as the doctor carried Emily out to the car. "Things should be livening up about then."

Neil looked up at the sky. The snow had almost stopped, though a few stray flakes were still drifting down.

"I hope you don't get stuck," he said.

"Don't worry," Dr. Harvey promised. "I'll get there. Even if I have to borrow a sleigh and harness Finn and Sandy!"

Back in the car, Carole turned for home.

"We'll drop Denny off on the way," she said. "It's a good thing it's not far."

The lights were on in the Wards' house when the Range Rover pulled up outside. Neil hurried up the path and rang the doorbell. Emily refused to stay in the car and hobbled after Nick and Carole who had brought Denny.

Beth Ward opened the door and stood frozen, staring at Denny by Nick's feet.

"Oh, it is!" she said at last. "Oh, thank you! You really found him."

"Beth?" It was Gina's voice. "Who are you —?"

She came up the passage behind Beth, and broke off as she saw Denny. The retriever bounded away from Nick, barking eagerly and licking Gina's face as she hugged him.

"Easy to see he's yours," Nick said, a bit sadly.

"But where did you find him?" Beth asked. "His collar's gone — and Emily, what happened to you? Oh, come in, everybody, and tell us all about it."

They all crowded into the Wards' tiny kitchen. Gina went to get her mother so she could hear the good news, while Beth found a chair for Emily. Neil let Jake and Sam roam around while he and Emily told the story, with additions now and again from their mother and Nick.

"So it's *you* we've really got to thank," Mrs. Ward said to Nick, when they had finished. "I'm sure Denny would have frozen to death if you hadn't looked after him. You bad boy!" she added to Denny. "Don't you dare wander off like that again!"

Denny, with his face in a bowl of food, didn't seem too bothered by the scolding. Mrs. Ward took out her purse and took out all of her cash, which she held out to Nick.

"Don't be offended," she said. "But I'm sure you can make good use of this. And Denny's worth ten times as much to us."

Nick grinned. "I don't offend easy, ma'am." He took the money and stowed it away inside his ragged overcoat. "Thanks. It was a pleasure to look after him. He's a wonderful dog."

"He's really clever!" Emily said. "Beth, show Nick some of Denny's tricks."

Denny had finished eating, so Beth snapped her

fingers to get his attention, shook hands with him, and made him beg for a biscuit and jump over her outstretched arm.

"It's silly to think he doesn't enjoy it," Emily said.

"I wouldn't force him," Beth said, petting Denny and rewarding him with a biscuit. "All right, trouble, here you are," she added to Jake, who trotted up to her and pushed his nose into her hand. She gave him a biscuit, and one to Sam, who had better manners, but was looking on hopefully. "At least now we can forget about that awful phone call. It wasn't anything to do with animal rights at all."

"Glen told us none of his friends would steal a dog," said Emily.

"So all we have to worry about now is the show," said Gina.

"Will it still go on?" Neil asked.

"Yes, of course it will!" Beth sounded cheerful and determined. "We've still got a week. Now that Denny's back we can do anything! Emily, I'll give you a call about rehearsals after Christmas, OK?"

"But I've hurt my ankle," Emily said. Neil could see she was trying hard not to cry. "I can't be in it."

"Oh, yes, you can," said Beth. "I'm not having you drop out now — not when you've done so much to get Denny back."

"Dr. Harvey says I shouldn't walk on it."

"Then you can do your part sitting down." Beth

refused to be put off. "Don't worry, I'll work it out. You can still sing, can't you?"

Emily started to smile, even though she had to wipe away a tear or two. Neil and the others pretended not to notice.

"And another thing, Neil," Beth went on. "I've been thinking. When we do the show, there are a lot of scenes where Denny isn't on. I've got too much to do to look after him myself, and so has Gina, so I need somebody to be responsible for him. How would you like to be the show's official dog handler?"

Neil stared at her. He'd resigned himself to being out of the performance altogether. Now he was so pleased he thought he was going to burst.

"Dog handler?" he echoed. "You bet! That's what I do best!"

On the way home, the roads were dark and silent. Very few cars were out. Carole drove slowly and carefully. The snow gleamed an eerie white in the car headlights. At long last the Range Rover turned into the drive of King Street Kennels.

"Made it!" said Carole.

As she switched off the engine, the front door opened and Bob came down the steps.

"Are you all right?" he asked. "What took so long?"

Carole passed a hand over her face. Neil thought that she looked tired.

"It's a long story," she said. "I'll tell you in a few

minutes. Can you take Emily indoors while we put this dog food away?"

"Sure." Bob swung Emily up into his arms and carried her off up the steps into the house. Neil thought he hadn't even noticed Nick.

Everyone else got out of the car. Neil had to give Sam a shove from behind; the Border collie had fallen asleep during the drive, but Neil thought he was none the worse for the whole ordeal. He followed Neil through the side gate, while Carole and Nick unloaded the cases of dog food Carole had bought at the Cash-and-Carry.

Neil went to open up the storeroom for his mother and Nick to begin stacking boxes, but the room already looked full.

"The Preston's van must have come," Carole said, pushing a strand of hair out of her eyes. "Wouldn't you just know! I didn't have to go to the Cash-and-Carry at all."

"And then we wouldn't have found Denny," Neil pointed out. "Or Nick."

From his cozy nest in Neil's jacket, Jake gave a little yap of agreement.

"All right, boy," Neil said affectionately. "We all know you really found him."

It didn't take long for the extra food to be stored away and Carole to close up the storeroom. Nick said to her, "I see you've got a barn, ma'am."

"That's right."

"Maybe I could sleep there, instead of in the house? I don't feel right under a roof. I haven't slept in a regular bed for years."

"Well . . ."

Carole was hesitating, but Neil thought Nick's idea was a really good one. The barn was partially heated, and there was plenty of straw there, kept for the dogs' bedding. Nick could have blankets and a sleeping bag from the house. Now that he thought about it, Neil wouldn't have minded spending the night there himself.

"Emily will be pleased," he said. "She won't have to share with Squirt."

"Well, Nick, if it's really what you'd prefer . . ." Carole said.

Nick's creased smile reappeared. "That'd be just great, ma'am."

As they crossed the courtyard to the back door, Bob appeared. He bent down, stroked Sam's head, and felt for his heartbeat.

"Seems OK," he said, "but it wasn't a good idea to take him out like that, Neil. We'll keep an eye on him for a day or two, and if there seems to be a problem we'll call Mike."

He let Sam go, and the Border collie slipped past him into the house. Bob shook hands with Nick.

"Hello. Emily told me you looked after Denny. Welcome to King Street. I hear you're spending Christmas with us?"

"Seems like it, sir." Nick touched his forehead as if he might have lifted his cap to Bob. "And your wife says I might help out with the dogs. I love dogs."

"That's fine, Nick. I'm sure we can find you some odd jobs to do."

While Nick and Bob were talking, Carole was tapping her foot impatiently. "Bob," she said, "do you think we could all go inside and get warm?"

"Yes — yes, of course." For the first time Neil thought his father was looking agitated. Surely nothing else could go wrong now? "You see the Preston's delivery came?" his dad asked, still standing in the doorway. "Not long ago. I'd just about given up on them."

"Yes, Bob," Carole said, starting to sound irritated. "But do we have to talk about it out here?"

"And there was an e-mail." Now Neil was sure his dad was talking for the sake of talking. What was there inside the house that he didn't want Carole to see? "An e-mail from John Cartwright," Bob went on wildly. "He wishes us a Merry Christmas, and he says he's enjoying the sun, but it really isn't the same without Bernie. Next year he says he's going to be spending Christmas with his best friend."

Neil had to think about that, even while he wondered about his dad's strange behavior. He'd imagined how pleased John Cartwright would be if he had managed to make Bernie into a real rescue dog. But he'd failed so far. And now he realized that Bernie was already much more special than just another rescue dog. He was John Cartwright's best friend. Bernie didn't *need* any extra training.

"Bob," said Carole, with exaggerated patience, "why are we standing on the back step in the freezing cold talking about John Cartwright's e-mail?"

Bob looked sheepish. "There's something I should tell you —"

He grabbed at Carole's arm as she headed past him, missed, and made a face at Neil as they all trooped into the kitchen with Carole in the lead. Neil almost slammed into his mom as she halted in the doorway.

"Bob!" she said. "What have you done?"

Peering around his mom, Neil stared into the kitchen. It was warm and bright. Delicious cooking smells were wafting from huge pots on top of the stove. At the kitchen table Emily was seated, with her injured foot on a stool. Sarah was sitting on the floor beside Sam's basket. Both had beaming smiles on their faces. But none of that was what made Neil stare.

The kitchen was full of dogs. Sam was in his basket. Two tiny white puppies, younger even than Jake, were scrambling all over Sarah and licking her face. A bull terrier with a white clown-face peered around the side of the old basket chair by the window. An Afghan hound, elegant and long-haired, was sprawled over most of the free floor space, while a black Scottie sat beside Emily, stumpy tail wagging as she scratched his wiry coat.

Carole blinked. "Bob — tell me I'm dreaming."

"Sorry," said Bob.

"These are the rescue dogs. What are they all doing in here?"

"That's what I was trying to tell you. The heating has gone off in the rescue center, and I don't know what the problem is. And I won't be able to get a mechanic out here until after Christmas." He spread his arms open. "I had to put them somewhere."

But Bob . . ." Carole still looked appalled. "Bob, I've invited Alex Harvey for Christmas. He's bringing Finn and Sandy as well."

"More dogs!" Sarah was delighted. "Lots of dogs for Christmas!"

Suddenly Carole's laughter bubbled up. She stood there shaking with it.

"If this is a dog's life," she gasped out when she could speak again, "then I can't get enough of it!"

Bob gave her a hug and went to start serving dinner. Neil picked his way around all the dogs to put Jake down beside Sam, and then got some food and water. He was turning back around with the full bowls when he saw that Jake had grabbed Bob's slipper and was shaking it fiercely, growling and gnawing with tiny teeth.

"That's right, Jake," Neil said. "Save us from Dad's killer stinky slipper!"

He grinned across the kitchen at Emily, who grinned back.

"This is going to be a great Christmas," she said.

"A great Christmas," Neil agreed. "A real, doggy, Puppy Patrol Christmas!"